Special Thanks

Kaely would like to thank her mother, Terri Moore, who supported her own exploration of Yellowstone, and who gave Buff a name. She would also like to thank the hot tour guide turned park ranger, Lucas Ross, who is her everyday inspiration.

Vanora would like to thank her friends for all the support and enthusiasm they have shown for this project. Heather Galanty and Cheri Bowman for their input, advice and encouragement, thank you!

Lastly we would both like to thank the Yellowstone Savages who made our seasonal experiences unique and truly amazing. Lupine!

Buff The Bison Explores
Yellowstone

By Kaely Moore

The morning dawned bright and clear, with streaks of color painted across the sky. A young bison, with thick reddish fur and four scrawny legs, stretched in a patch of golden sunlight and shook his head to rid it of sleep. He blinked his big, black eyes at the pink and purple sunrise, looking across the rushing river and a great, green valley.

This bison's name was Buff, and he lived in Yellowstone National Park. He didn't know for sure, but he thought that it might just be the most beautiful place in the whole world.

Today looked like most other days to Buff. The grass was sparkling with dew and the tall lodgepole pine trees stood quiet and still on the hillside.

But today was not like other days. Today, the herd was on the move, and Buff was finally going to explore his home.

His mother and the older bison in the herd had told all of the calves stories about the strange and amazing sights in Yellowstone. Buff knew about the hot water that sprayed from the ground and the boiling pools in every color he could imagine. But he hadn't seen any of them yet, and he couldn't wait to get started.

He darted over to his sleeping mother and woke her with a quick nudge against her dark brown, furry head. Buff's mama, Ralphie, was a lot bigger than he was. As she stood and stomped one of her heavy hooves, a cloud of dust rose around them.

"Mama!" Buff cried. "It's today! We get to see the park today!"

Mama sighed, breathing out through her large, black nose. She had seen all of Yellowstone many times, but it was still new to Buff. She could tell he was very excited, and it made her happy.

"Yes, Buff," she said, nuzzling his head with her own. "It is today. Let's join the rest of the herd. It looks like they are about to head out."

The two bison made their way over to the group, which was gathering in the shadow of National Park Mountain. Buff sped up as they got closer, and tumbled into his best friend, Loe.

Loe was the same age as Buff, and just as excited to see Yellowstone. She got to her feet and snorted. "Hey!" she said. "I'll get you back for that one!"

"I'm sure you will," Buff answered. "But it was fun anyway!"

Mama caught up with the calves and the herd took a quick look around to make sure everyone was there. Then they set off to walk south along the Firehole River.

The Firehole was a very pretty river, with clear water that sparkled when the sun hit it. As they walked, the herd spotted other animals in the water and between the trees.

"Those are swans," Mama said, nodding toward two large white birds drifting in the river. They had big wings with smooth feathers and bright orange and black bills.

"And what is that?" Buff asked, looking to the top of a nearby hillside. He had spotted a gray dog that was watching them as they passed. It had a bushy tail and big, pointed ears.

"That is a coyote," Mama said. "They are clever animals that live with us here in the park. Sometimes you can hear them howling to each other at night."

"Are they dangerous?" Buff asked nervously.

"Not to us, no. We have more to fear from the wolves, who are much larger. And even then, they are only truly dangerous when we are alone, which is why it is very important that we stick together."

Buff stepped a little closer to Mama.

The herd stopped to take a quick drink of water from the river, and then kept walking until they got to a place where the earth turned black and very hard.

"Okay, you two," Mama began, "I need you to walk on one side of me. Stay close, and follow the trees."

"What's wrong, Mama?" Buff asked.

"We are at the road," she answered. "It is a piece of land that the humans have made to travel through the park. Sometimes we use it, too. But we have to be careful. The humans often forget that we are much bigger than they are, and they get closer than they should."

Loe glanced quickly at Buff, and he could tell she was scared.

"Will they hurt us, Ralphie?" she asked.

"Hmmm," Mama said. "I don't think so. But the herd has to stay aware, just in case. Don't worry, Loe. We will always keep you safe."

Buff suddenly felt very small. He had seen a few humans before, but they were always far away. He wished he was big enough to protect himself. Big like his dad, Smoky, who was strong and could leave the herd on his own.

When he grew up, Buff would be able to run as fast as a grizzly bear. He could use his horns and his tough hooves to scare away wolves. And he would be able to jump clear over the head of a full-grown human. He couldn't wait!

As the bison continued down the road, Buff started to smell something very strange. It wasn't too strong at first, but soon it seemed to surround them, and Buff tried to bury his nose in Mama's fur.

"It smells like something is rotting!" he cried.

Next to him, he watched as Loe took a deep breath of air, and let it out slowly. "I like it!" she said happily. "It's weird, but in a good way."

Buff thought she was crazy. This smell made him feel sick to his stomach.

"It's sulfur," Mama told them. "That smell is sulfur, and it tells us that we are getting closer to the thermal features. You'll get used to it, Buff," she said warmly.

Buff forgot the smell for just a moment. "Thermal features?" he said. "What do you mean?"

"I mean," Mama began, "that you are about to see one reason why Yellowstone is such a very special place."

Buff felt his tail twitch with excitement, and he walked a little faster.

"A large part of our home sits on top of a very old, very big volcano," Mama went on. "This volcano, full of fire and ash and melted stone, erupted a long time ago, and someday it will erupt again. All through the park, we can see signs that the volcano is still alive beneath our feet. The clearest signs are in the thousands of thermal features here in Yellowstone.

"Thermal," she added, "means heat."

"Do you hear that?" Loe said suddenly, stopping in her tracks. The three bison got very quiet. And then, Buff heard it, too.

Bloop.
Bloop, gloop.
Gloop, bloop, bloop.

"Ah," Mama said, leading them forward again, "we have reached the mud pots."

The herd wandered off the road a bit and followed a trail made out of wood that the humans had created to keep from touching the ground. Mama explained that humans did not have hooves to protect their feet, so they built paths to help them see the thermal features more safely.

Tall trees grew on each side of the trail, with white roots that were hard as stone. The trees had soaked up water from the soil near thermal features, and the minerals in the water had turned them white. Mama told them that the humans called these "Bobby Sock Trees," named after the silly pieces of cloth they put on their feet to keep them warm.

The bison came upon a shallow hole about the size of a small pond. On all sides of it, there were pieces of wood stacked together to make what Mama said was called a "fence." She hopped over it easily, but Buff and Loe were too small, so they had to squeeze between the wooden boards.

Buff gasped at what he saw on the other side. The ground seemed to be moving!

After taking a closer look, he realized that he was standing at the edge of a bubbling pool of mud. It looked thick, and more colorful than normal mud, with swirls of white, gray and pink. The bubbles grew as fast as they burst, some even popping out of dried, cracked mounds just outside of the pool. Buff couldn't take his eyes off of the strange sight.

"Wow," Loe said softly. "Why is it smoking?" she asked, looking at the thin, white clouds rising slowly from the top of the pool.

"That is not smoke, dear," Mama said. "It's called steam, and it happens when liquids like water get very hot."

Buff inched closer to the mud for a better look. The pool didn't seem too deep, and he wondered what it would be like to jump into it.

"Can I touch it, Mama?" he asked.

"No, Buff," Mama said, and her voice got serious. "The heat underground has mixed with water, and has broken down the rocks here to make dangerous chemicals that can hurt you very badly. This is not the kind of mud you can play in."

Buff sighed. He still thought it looked like fun.

"Come on," Mama said. "It's getting late, and we need to find a place to sleep tonight."

Buff had not noticed how low the sun was in the sky, or how long their shadows had gotten. He was starting to feel tired now.

The herd walked a little further along the road, and then settled down beside it in a wide, grassy meadow. Buff could hear crickets chirping softly all around them.

Loe said goodnight before trotting away to find her own mother, and Buff curled up next to Mama. Nights in Yellowstone could get very chilly, but Mama's heavy fur always kept him warm.

The sun set behind the hills in the west, and Buff looked up at the sky to greet the billions of friendly stars that lived there.

"Goodnight, Mama," he yawned.

Mama rested her head beside his. "Goodnight, Buff," she said.

They woke up the next morning to thick fog hanging low over the road. Buff sniffed the air carefully. He could still smell the sulfur, but it wasn't as strong as before. Maybe Mama was right, he thought, and he was starting to get used to it.

"Where are we going today?" he asked, as Mama slowly chewed the long grass at their feet.

"Today, we will keep heading south," she said knowingly. "And I think the park will have a few more surprises for us along the way."

Buff was eager to get the day started. He couldn't wait to see what else they might discover!

Soon enough, the herd took off into the fog, wandering through the trees along the road. Buff couldn't see very far in front of him, so he made sure to stay close to Mama.

Overhead, two big, black ravens hopped from branch to branch, squawking loudly at one another. Buff snorted. He thought that ravens could be very pretty birds if they weren't so annoying. Every time he saw them, they seemed to be fighting about something.

One of the ravens above them now had a small, shiny object clamped in her long, pointed beak, and she didn't want to share it with her friend.

"It's mine, Edgar!" the raven shouted, her voice muffled by the prize she carried. "It's for my nest! Go get your own!"

"Your nest has enough things in it!" the other raven said. "You are so selfish, Lena! Just give it to me!"

"What are they even arguing over?" Buff asked, trying to get a look at the object.

Mama glanced up to see what he was talking about. "I don't know," she said. "It might be something the humans made."

"Ravens are smart animals," she went on. "If humans leave their things sitting around for too long, those birds usually find a way to snatch them up."

Ravens did not sound very nice to Buff, and he was happy to leave them behind.

As they continued their journey, the fog began to break apart and the sun shone down warmly between the clouds. The smell of sulfur was much stronger now, and Buff could hear a loud rushing of water. He knew that Yellowstone had many beautiful waterfalls, and he wondered if there was one nearby.

When they finally got to the source of the sound, Buff was fairly certain they had just found the strangest waterfall there ever was. This waterfall was steaming, and the rocks behind it were yellow and orange!

"Mama!" Buff cried, stopping to watch the water as it poured endlessly into the Firehole River, so close to the road where they stood. "What's wrong with that waterfall, Mama?"

Mama pushed him forward lightly with her nose. "There is nothing wrong with it," she said. "But it's not really a waterfall. It's called 'runoff water,' and it comes from a giant thermal feature. Would you like to see it?"

Buff nodded his head without another word. He definitely wanted to see it.

They cut across a shallow part of the river, following the herd through the cool water and up the hill on the other side.

When they got to the top, Buff couldn't believe his eyes. He was looking down into a deep, blue pool. It was wider than the river they had just crossed, and it was deep enough to hold the whole herd. The water was the clearest blue he had ever seen, and great big clouds of white steam floated up from it. Buff thought it looked like the sky had turned upside down, and it made him a little dizzy.

"The humans call this 'Excelsior'," Mama said. "Every day, hot runoff water from this pool gushes into the Firehole River. Because of this, and run-off from other thermal features in the park, the river is sometimes very warm."

Buff did not want to move from this spot. He could stand here forever, looking into that beautiful blue water. But Mama had other plans.

"Come," she said. "This is quite pretty, but there is something else I want to show you."

Mama told Buff to watch his step as they walked around the steep edge of Excelsior.

"It would be a very long fall into boiling hot water!" she reminded him. "Please be safe!"

Buff kept a close eye on where he set down each of his four hooves. A long fall into any kind of water did not sound like fun to him.

After a few steps, Buff started to see changes in the ground beneath him. At first, the earth was hard and white. But slowly, the colors began to transform. The bison crossed over small streams of water where the ground was dark brown. Soon, each of Buff's careful steps came with a squish as his hooves sunk into land that was soft, wet and orange.

"What do you think?" Mama asked, pausing suddenly. Buff came to a stop next to her and lifted his eyes to see what she was talking about.

A gigantic, circular rainbow seemed to be spread out on the ground in front of them. Its colors went from the orange where they stood, to rings of yellow and green, and a deep, dark blue center. It was a pool so big that Buff couldn't see the other side of it.

"It's amazing!" he said. "What is it?"

"This is Grand Prismatic," Mama explained. "It is the biggest hot spring in all of Yellowstone."

"Can we go closer?" Buff asked.

"No," Mama said. "This is as close as we can go. The colors of this spring, like the colors at the runoff water we saw by the river, help us to see how dangerous it might be," she went on. "The colors are caused by tiny creatures that we can't even see. Humans call them bacteria. These creatures live in the hot water from thermal features. They make different colors in different temperatures of water."

"So, the bacteria that look orange," Buff began, "live in water that is not as hot?"

"Exactly," Mama said. "It is still very warm, but we can step here. The water gets hotter the closer you move to the middle of the pool. There are different bacteria that live where the water is yellow and green, and the temperature is higher. Not much can survive where it becomes blue. It is simply much too hot."

29

Buff stood staring at the quiet ripples on the pool's surface. The wind blew a huge billow of steam over their path, and he could see the colors of Grand Prismatic reflected softly in the white cloud.

There was another wooden trail nearby like the one they had followed at the mud pots. Buff didn't notice it before, but now he saw that it was crowded with humans. They came in all sorts of shapes, sizes and colors. Some were very old, and others were very young. Buff had never seen so many of them! He wasn't sure if he should be scared by all of these new and strange faces.

But they didn't look scary, he thought. They were all staring at the same thing he was staring at. And they all looked just as excited about this big, beautiful hot spring as he was. This was a peaceful place, Buff decided, where everyone could come and be amazed.

Just then, something brown and heavy slammed into Buff's side, sending him crashing to the squishy, orange ground.

"Oof!" he cried. "What was that?"

He looked up to see Loe standing over him and looking quite proud of herself.

"I told you I would get you back!" she said.

Buff got to his feet and shook out his wet fur. "Yeah," he said, "I guess you did." He bumped her playfully with his shoulder. "That doesn't mean I have to like it, though!"

Mama snorted. She did not look happy.

"You both need to be more careful," she told them. "Thermal features are not places to play around. Even here, where the ground looks safe, it can be very weak. There are areas in the park where bison have broken through the surface and gotten badly burned by hot water that flows underground."

Loe hung her head. "I'm sorry, Ralphie," she said. "I didn't know."

"It's okay, Loe." Mama's voice softened. "You were having fun. Just remember to be safe, too."

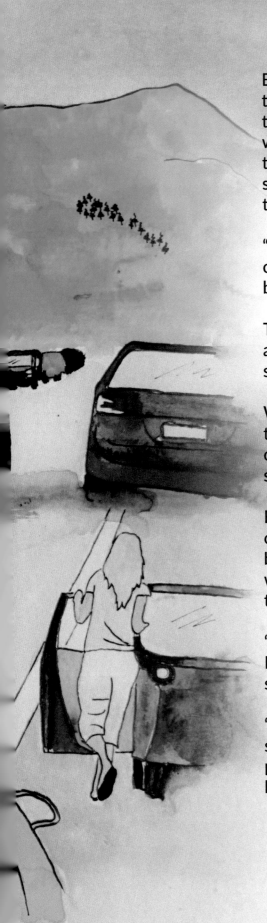

Buff and Loe followed Mama in silence as the herd turned back toward the road. Buff watched Mama's tail swish back and forth while they walked, and he wondered about what she had told them. He knew that Yellowstone was full of wonders, but he was still just learning about how dangerous some of those wonders could be.

"We have one more stop to make today!" Mama called back to them. "Stay close, because there will be many more humans where we are headed next!"

The two calves looked nervously at one another, and then sped up to walk beside Mama. They were soon very glad they did.

When they reached the road again, the herd found that it was now lined with big, noisy machines made out of metal. The humans called them cars, Mama said, and they used them to move around the park.

Buff watched as face after face poked curiously out of car windows to get a closer look at the passing bison. They were much too close, he thought. Some were even stopping to get out and walk toward them!

"Mama!" Buff cried. "Mama, what should we do?" He and Loe had pushed up against Mama's side, suddenly frightened.

"Don't worry, you two," Mama said. Her body seemed tense, but her voice was calm. "There is a park ranger up ahead. He will make sure the other humans don't get closer than they should."

Buff looked down the road. He saw a human man speaking to the people nearby. This man wore a funny hat and a friendly smile. As he spoke, the other humans stopped moving forward.

"What is a park ranger?" Loe asked.

"They are humans who care very much about Yellowstone," Mama said. "They help to protect it, to protect us, and to protect the other humans who come here."

Buff felt his body relax a bit, and he stopped trying to
hide himself in Mama's fur. The humans stayed back
far enough to let the herd cross the road and disappear
into the trees on the other side.

Park rangers seemed very helpful, Buff thought. None
of those humans looked like they would do anything
to hurt him, but so many of them all at once made him
nervous. It was good that there were rangers around to
keep everyone safe.

The sun was again drooping low in the sky, and Buff's legs were starting to get tired. They had done a lot of walking over the past two days!

"Are we almost there?" Loe asked. Buff wondered if she had read his mind. He looked over to see that Loe looked just as tired as he felt. Her hooves were dragging slowly through the dirt at their feet.

"Almost," said a soft voice right behind them. Loe's mother, Laurel, had joined their group. She gave Loe a light bump with her nose to keep her moving. "Wake up, little one," she said. "You will not want to miss your first geyser eruption!"

A geyser! Buff was suddenly wide awake. He knew all about the geysers from Mama's stories. They were almost like hot springs, but something in them was squeezed tight underground. Instead of water flowing freely to the surface, it built up and then erupted in great fountains of water that sprayed from the ground to touch the sky. He couldn't believe he was actually going to see one!

"Come on!" Buff said, poking Loe with his nose until she gave him a very annoyed look. "It will be dark soon, and we won't be able to see it!" he explained. "Let's go!"

Loe sighed and picked up the pace as Buff broke into a trot. He hopped over stones and logs in his path, and skidded to a sudden stop at the top of a small hill.

Quiet clouds of steam rose from the earth in soft, white pillars as far as Buff's eyes could see. Their old friend, the Firehole River, cut a smooth path through a valley that seemed to be covered in thermal features. Buff wanted to move, but he had no idea where to go!

"Are those all geysers?" he asked when Mama and the others had caught up to him.

"Not all of them," Laurel said. "But there are definitely a lot. This is the Upper Geyser Basin, and it is home to hundreds of geysers, hot springs and steam vents."

"W-which one are we going to see?" Loe said with a giant yawn.

Mama took the lead down the hill. "We are going to see Old Faithful, the most famous geyser in Yellowstone," she said. "It looks like there are already quite a few humans gathered around to watch, so hopefully it will erupt soon."

Buff saw what she was talking about as they set off across a wide clearing toward the river. There were humans everywhere! Some of them were walking along wooden trails nearby. And past the Firehole, he could see crowds of people sitting together on benches that circled one of the steady streams of gently rising steam.

That must be it, he thought. Old Faithful!

The bison splashed through the river and scrambled up a grassy hill on the other side. They kept their distance from the humans, and settled down to wait near the rocky mound of Old Faithful's cone.

Buff's eyes stayed fixed on the steam puffing into the air. Every once in a while, the geyser would bubble and gurgle and spray. Water sloshed up from inside the cone, but only a little bit.

Buff was fooled every time. He was so excited that he inched closer for the big moment.

"Not too close, Buff," Mama reminded him. "Stay safe, remember?"

Buff stomped one of his hooves and took a step back. He didn't think he could wait any longer!

Something bumped his shoulder, and he looked over to see Loe standing next to him.

"Hey," she said. Her eyes looked droopy and tired, but he could tell that she was excited, too.

"Hey," Buff said back. He was glad that she was here.

They turned toward Old Faithful just as the geyser started to bubble again. Buff held his breath. Was this it?

It was!

The eruption started slow at first, with low bursts of water that sloshed and splashed. And then, those bursts got taller, rising higher and higher until a tower of water scraped the darkening sky above them.

A great rushing sound filled the air, and Buff felt a light mist as the water fell back to the earth. Droplets clung to his fur like rain, and he kicked out his back hooves with joy.

The eruption only lasted a few minutes. They watched the tower shrink back, and Old Faithful's cone once again began to belch steam. Buff thought this must be the most wonderful few minutes of his life.

"Wow," Loe gasped. She sounded stunned. "That was cool."

"That was fantastic!" Buff cried. He turned toward Mama. "So, we just saw the best geyser in all of Yellowstone?" he asked her.

"Well," she began, shaking the mist out of her fur, "you saw the most famous geyser in all of Yellowstone. Old Faithful is well known because it goes off quite often, and we can usually guess when it will erupt again based on the last time it did," she went on.

"But there are hundreds of geysers here in the park, and some of them are even bigger than this one! You should probably see a few more before you decide which one you think is the best."

"Oh," Buff said. He couldn't imagine anything better than what he just saw, but he was ready to find it. "Okay. Well, let's go then!" He started off back toward the river and the pillars of steam that waited for him on the other side.

"Hold on there, Buff!" Mama said, stopping him in his tracks. "It has been a long couple of days, and this one is almost over." She nodded at the setting sun. "You need some rest. Tomorrow will be another good day to explore Yellowstone."

Mama touched her nose to his, and he sighed. "Alright," he said. He wanted to see more geysers, but he was very tired.

The herd had spread out through the valley in search of grass and a good place to sleep for the night. Buff and Mama stayed close to Loe and Laurel, lying down in a patch of trees that overlooked the geyser basin. The last rays of golden sun made the ground glitter, and Buff watched clouds of steam rise up to meet the stars.

As he fell into a deep sleep, curled up next to Mama, Buff felt sure that Yellowstone really was the most beautiful place in the whole world.

The End

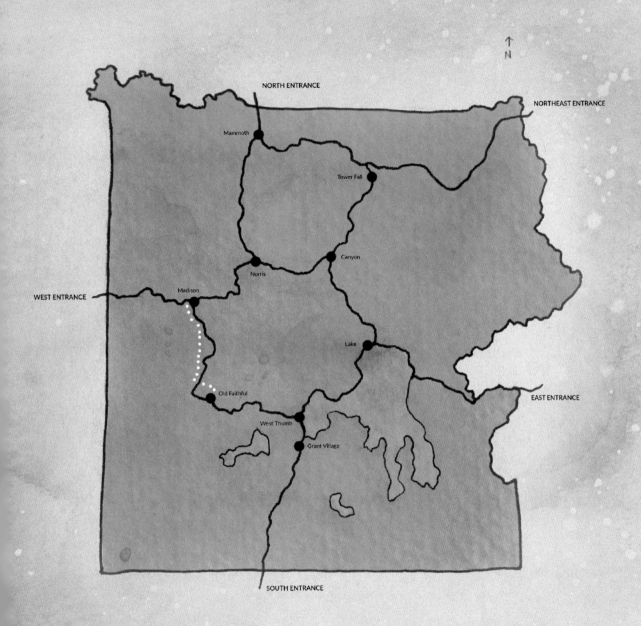

NORTH ENTRANCE

NORTHEAST ENTRANCE

Mammoth

Tower Fall

Canyon

Norris

Madison

WEST ENTRANCE

Lake

Old Faithful

EAST ENTRANCE

West Thumb

Grant Village

SOUTH ENTRANCE

↑
N

Made in the USA
Middletown, DE
07 June 2021